CLIFFORD®

FOUR FAVORITE STORIES

Clifford the Small Red Puppy
Clifford the Big Red Dog
Clifford's Birthday Party
Clifford Goes to Hollywood

SCHOLASTIC INC.

New York Toronto London Auckland Sydney
Mexico City New Delhi Hong Kong Buenos Aires

Clifford the Small Red Puppy (0-590-44294-5)
Copyright © 1972 by Norman Bridwell.

Clifford the Big Red Dog (0-590-44297-X)
Copyright © 1963, 1985 by Norman Bridwell.

Clifford's Birthday Party (0-590-44279-1)
Copyright © 1988 by Norman Bridwell.

Clifford Goes to Hollywood (0-590-44289-9)
Copyright © 1980 by Norman Bridwell.

All rights reserved. Published by Scholastic Inc.
SCHOLASTIC, CARTWHEEL BOOKS, and associated logos
are trademarks and/or registered trademarks of Scholastic Inc.

ISBN 0-439-84800-8

10 9 8 7 6 5 4 3 2   6 7 8 9 10 11/0
Printed in Singapore 46 • This collection first printing, June 2006

CLIFFORD®

THE SMALL
RED PUPPY

Story and pictures by Norman Bridwell

To Amy, Melissa, Beth, and Debbie

Hi! I'm Emily Elizabeth
and this is Clifford, my big red dog.

Yesterday my friend Martha said,
"I got my dog from a fancy pet store.
Where did you get yours?"

So I told her how I got Clifford.

When I was little I lived in the city.
I didn't have a dog.

One day the man down the hall called us.
His dog had puppies. He wanted to give me one.

One puppy was smaller than the rest.

The man said, "Don't take him. He is the runt.
He will always be small and sick."
But I loved that little puppy. He needed me.

I named my puppy Clifford.
He was so tiny that I had to feed him
with the doll's baby bottle.

We got the smallest collar we could find
for Clifford.

It was too big.

When he began to eat dog food,
we had to watch him all the time.

He was so little that he was always getting lost, even in our small apartment.

Daddy said Clifford was just too small.
He didn't think he could live through the
winter. I was very sad.

That night I told Clifford I wished he
would grow to be a big healthy dog.
I told him I loved him.

Next morning he looked bigger to me.

He seemed to have an easier time
eating his dog food.

And his collar wasn't so loose.

In fact, by the time Daddy got home
the collar was too small.

By bedtime Clifford's tiny basket
seemed a little too small for him.

So I let him sleep on my pillow again.

That was a mistake.

Next morning Mommy thought
Clifford looked different.
Daddy said, "I think he is growing."

I decided to take Clifford for a walk.
At the corner I saw a big dog coming.
I knew I should pick Clifford up
so the big dog couldn't hurt him.

I shouldn't have worried.

Clifford really was growing!
We ran home to show Mommy how big he was.

Had our apartment door grown smaller?

Daddy couldn't believe it. We put Clifford
in the garden to sleep that night.

In the morning the lady upstairs called us.
It was about Clifford.

In fact, all the neighbors
were starting to notice him.

The landlord called the police.
They came to see Clifford.
They said Clifford would have to go.
But how? He couldn't go through the door.

There was just one way to get him
out of our garden.

We sent him to live with my uncle
who lived in the country.

I was sad. I missed my little puppy.

And he missed me.

One day we got a surprise.
My uncle wanted Daddy to come work
with him in the country.
We moved right away.

Clifford was waiting for me.

I said, "Clifford, stop growing.

You are just right."

"So," I said to Martha,
"that's how I got my dog.
Tell me how you got your dog."

Martha said, "Forget it."

CLIFFORD®
THE BIG RED DOG

For the real Emily Elizabeth

CLIFFORD®
THE BIG RED DOG

Story and pictures by Norman Bridwell

I'm Emily Elizabeth,
and I have a dog.

My dog is a big red dog.

Other kids I know have dogs, too.
Some are big dogs.

And some are red dogs.

But I have the biggest, reddest dog on our street.

This is my dog — Clifford.

We have fun together. We play games.

I throw a stick, and he
brings it back to me.

He makes mistakes sometimes.

We play hide-and-seek.

I'm a good hide-and-seek player.

I can find Clifford,
no matter where he hides.

We play camping out,
and I don't need a tent.

He can do tricks, too.
He can sit up and beg.

Oh, I know he's not perfect.
He has *some* bad habits.

He runs after cars.
He chases some of them.

He runs after cats, too.
We don't go to the zoo anymore.

He digs up flowers.

Clifford loves to chew shoes.

It's not easy to keep Clifford.
He eats and drinks a lot.

His house was a problem, too.

But he's a very good watchdog.

The bad boys don't come around anymore.

One day I gave Clifford a bath.

And I combed his hair,
and took him to the dog show.

I'd like to say Clifford won first prize.
But he didn't.

I don't care.

You can keep all your small dogs.

You can keep all your black,

white, brown, and spotted dogs.

I'll keep Clifford.... Wouldn't you?

CLIFFORD'S
BIRTHDAY PARTY

Norman Bridwell

For Adam, James, and Patrick

My name is Emily Elizabeth,
and this is my dog Clifford.
Last week was Clifford's birthday.
We invited his pals to a party.

Mom had ice cream and cookies.
We put up decorations.

When it was time for the party to begin,
nobody was there.
Where could they be?

We went looking for Clifford's pals.

They were all together at the playground.

I asked them why they hadn't come to the party.

Jenny said they wanted to come,
but they didn't have very good presents for Clifford —
not good enough for such a special friend.

I told them not to be silly.

Clifford would like whatever they got for him.

They all ran home to get their gifts...

and everyone came to the party.

First we opened the gift from Scott
and his dog Susie.
Scott had blown it up as much as he could.

Clifford blew it up some more.

We really had a ball.

Then Clifford pulled out the stopper.

That was a mistake.

The next gift was from Sam and his dog Lenny.
It was a piñata!

We hung the piñata from a tree.

There were treats inside for all the dogs.

Clifford was supposed to break the piñata
with a stick.
He gave a couple of good swings...

and the piñata broke open.

The dogs liked the treats...

but we decided not to give Clifford any more piñatas.

We all laughed when we saw the gift from
Jenny and her dog Flip.
It was a little small for Clifford.

But it was just right for his nose.
Clifford hates having a cold nose.

Alisha and Nero's gift was a toy dog that talked.

Clifford thought it was cute.
He went to pet it.

Uh-oh:

They don't make toys the way they used to.

It was time for ice cream when Cynthia
and her dog Basker arrived.

They brought Clifford a gift certificate
from the Bow Wow Beauty Parlor.
He could get a free shampoo and haircut.

We each had our own idea of how Clifford might look after the beauty parlor.

I like Clifford just the way he is.
I thanked Cynthia for the gift,
but I slipped the certificate to Scott
and Susie. I knew she would like it.

Then came the cake.

Clifford was surprised. He was even more surprised...

when his family popped out!

He hadn't seen his mother and father
and sisters and brother for a long time.

Clifford liked the presents his friends gave him,
but having his family and friends with him
was the best birthday present of all.

CLIFFORD®

GOES TO
HOLLYWOOD

Story and pictures by Norman Bridwell

To Lucinda Morgan Bailey

This is my dog, Clifford.
We do a lot of things together.

We swim together.

We play ball together.

In winter we go sliding together.

One day a man stopped us and asked
if Clifford would like to be in a movie.

Clifford had to take a screen test.
The man told him to act happy.

Clifford acted happy.

Then he asked him to act angry.

Then Clifford pretended to be in love.

The man told him to act frightened. He did.

Clifford acted sad.

The man said Clifford was a terrific actor.

He wanted him to be in a movie.

The next day they took Clifford to Hollywood.

We hated to see him go.

When the movie was finished, everybody said
Clifford was the best actor in the world.
Clifford was a star.

In Hollywood, they built him a big doghouse,
the kind a movie star should have.

They gave him fancy dishes
and brought him special things to eat.

Clifford's dog collars were made of gold
and expensive fur.
Some were covered with diamonds.

He even had a swimming pool
shaped like a bone.

Clifford loved being a star. They put his footprint
in the cement on Hollywood Boulevard, just like
the other stars.

Everywhere he went he was surrounded by mobs of movie fans.

They all wanted souvenirs.

His fans were everywhere.

There were a lot of parties. Clifford got tired
of them. But they said movie stars have to go
to a lot of parties.

I saw Clifford on a television talk show.
I thought he looked a little sad.

One day he looked over his wall and saw
a girl playing with her dog. He missed me.

Clifford was tired of being a star.
That night he jumped over the wall.

He left all the fancy dishes and collars
and parties behind.

Clifford came home! And he's home to stay.
He'd rather be with me than in Hollywood.

I'm glad he loves me as much as I love him.